Beyond the Mind is a collaborative writing project. The contributors are;

- Arran Milne

- Caitlin Lammie

- Finlay Mair

- Kyle Anderson

- Kym McAlpine

- Nathan Cooper

- Robbie Sneddon

- Sam Moon

- Sean Sharp

- Taylor Connolly

with cover design by Rowan Symington and Craig McNaughton. The project was overseen by Rachel Parker and Joe Reddington.

The group cheerfully acknowledges the wonderful help given by:

- Ruth McFarlane

- Peter Billington

- Angela Malcolm

- The English Department

- Lesley Smales

- Kerry Gibson

- Veronica Madden

- Derek Simpson

It's been a wonderful opportunity, and everyone involved has been filled with incredible knowledge and enthusiasm.

Finally, we would like to thank all staff at Queen Anne High School for their support in releasing our novelists from lessons for a full week.

The group started to plan out their novel at 9.15 on Monday 26 January 2015 and completed their last proof reading at 11.40 on Friday 30th January 2015.

We are incredibly proud to state that every word of the story, every idea, every chapter and yes, every mistake, is entirely their own work. No teachers, parents or other students touched a single key during this process, and we would ask readers to keep this in mind.

We are sure you will agree that this is an incredible achievement. It has been a true delight and privilege to see this group of young people turn into professional novelists in front of our very eyes.

Beyond the Mind

Tim Cooks

February 6, 2015

Contents

3

Chapter 1

Assessing Louis

Location: Doctors

Time: 05/02/201 - 7:10am

The doctors was old, dusty and mossy but it was still clean and

got lots of people still to get help and be healthy so they go to the doctors.

"You ok Louis you look nervous" As Gillian approached her

"Im just a wee bit worried at what dr baines is going to say"

"Don't worry Dr Baines is a nice guy hes got blue eyes he's quite tall and hes skinny "

"Theres no need, you'll be fine if you have a illness you will get better soon".

"We are here, you go sit down while I tell reception".

Gillian is a war veteran Gillian was fighting in "world war 3" Gillian is 81 years old Gillian was born on the 30th of August 1934. Sadly Gillian has PTSD and Gillian thinks there are soldiers in the room when there is nobody there, Gillian also has tourettes it makes her say stuff and shout out her personal thoughts. Gillian is a very friendly person and Gillian tells great stories.Louis the person at the desk said Dr Baines will be ready for us in ten minutes. "Meanwhile you just sit and relax or read one of those magazines". "stop fidgeting louis you'll be fine I promise" " I cant help it im just so nervous".

"Louis to see Dr Baines in room five"

"You ready"

"I guess so"

"Hi Louis im Dr Baines how are you what's the problem"

"well dr Baines i've been having these weird voices telling me what to do and asking me question about my life and how i'm doing but i'm still trying to work out who it is"

"ok just let me get my stuff sorted then ill do some tests ok".

"Louis im just going to do some tests on you to see if I can find out what's causing these voices. Louis can you fill out this sheet for me then we will get started. Thats great lets get started".

"So Gillian how are you"

"I was in world war z were you" "

yes I was"

"no way because I was in that war it was scarey but we got through it".

"John what did you do in the war"

"because i was head colonel"

"well I was a doctor helping the injured just

trying to do my bit to help out".

"When I was helping a guy to the shelter we were both shot at one of the bullets just missed my head by a very little margin after that, the guy was giving first aid and he survived".

"So Gillian maybe we could meet up some time and talk a bit more because right now we need to talk about Louis".

"Im afraid to tell you that Louis has got an illness but i'm afraid we still need to work out what it is but when we know I will call you straight away and ask you to come down and see me is that ok".

"Yes thankyou Doctor Baines".

"I'll get in touch when we know ok and if it keeps happening just come back

"Thanks again Dr Baines"

"Its my job"

"Now we just need to go home and get you rest".

Chapter 2

Assessing Gregg

Location: hospital

Time: 05/02/2014 - 08:10am

The hospital was really old dusty and covered in dirt.

Gregg and Gillian were waiting on the 32 princess street bus to go to the doctors. When they got on the 32 bus it was busy so Greg and Gillian had to stand. When Greg and Gillian got near the doc-

11

tors the bus broke down so Gregg and Gillian had to walk the rest of the way. Greggs appointment was at 3:10pm but Gregg and Gillian were going to be late. When Gregg and Gillian got there Gregg sat down while Gillian went up to the desk and told the woman at the counter who they were and they were late by 10 minutes.

Gregg and Gillian were sitting waiting for Dr Baines to call them it to asses Gregg. Gregg picked up a motorbike magazine and was reading it while Gillian was getting stressed waiting so they started to talk.

"So Greg are you ok you do not need to be scared"

"I'm not scared i'm just nervous about what hes going to say if there's something wrong with me"

"well you don't need to be, if you are ill then you dr baines will help you get better".

Greg and Gillian just sat quiet for the next five minutes.after five minutes they started talking again. After half an hour dr Baines was ready for them.

Dr Baines calls Gregg and Gillian,

"So Greg my name is dr baines I am a physiologist I can help you with your problems"

. "Hi Dr Baines".

"Gregg ill just get you to fill out this questionnaire about yourself". 10 minutes later Gregg had finished the questionnaire. dr baines went away and looked at the questionnaire for five minutes meanwhile gillion and Gregg sat and talked 5 minutes, later dr Baines came back.

"Gregg I will ask you some questions now about what is happening to you and how you have been feeling"

"What has been going on have you been seeing ghosts and dead people?"

"I have been seeing dead people, and they've been talking to me and its really scarey"

"you dont need to worry anymore because you will get better Gregg give me 5 minutes while I go and get some stuff to do tests and find out what the problem is ok".

"dr baines is this going to hurt"

"no greg its just a few tests on your brain"

clink Dr Baines opens a metal case.

"what's that "

"nothing Gregg its just my glasses"

Dr Baines takes him in for an x ray after 10 minutes hes back.

"Dr Baines what's wrong with him asked Gillian"

"I think you should sit down"

"ok now tell me".

Gregg has schizophrenia

"what is that"

"its a mental disorder and its if you can't tell if something is real or not"

"is there a cure dr baines"

" yes there is a cure Gregg would have to take these meds every day".

"will you give him the medicine".

"Greg we will be here all the time to talk to if the medicine is not working or if theres no difference at all then we will need to think of something else".

" Now Greg has to take this medicine, now hes to take 2 every day and when he runs out of them come back and get some more".

"Now greg you need to take these otherwise it won't get better and you'll keep suffering"

"Like I said before if they don't work then we will have to give you something else".

Gillion and Gregg are waiting on dr baines to bring back greggs prescription for when he runs out. "aahhhh dr baines thank you now do i bring this back here"

"yes thats so i know what stuff i gave you and what's wrong".

"So greg what are we going to do with you" dr baines asked .

"I don't know how long till the bus" asked Gregg

"10 minutes" Gillian replied

"Now gregg don't let anyone tease you at school or anywhere about what's wrong because it does not matter about what they think, what matters that you're getting better".

Gregg we will have to walk home because the bus is not coming. On the way home gregg starts to see dead people. Gillian asks him

" Gregg what's the matter"

" i'm seeing dead people right now" Greggs tells dr baines

"Try to block them out"

When they got home gregg had his dinner and went to his bed because he felt tired.

Chapter 3

Assessing Peter

Location: in the hospital

Time: 05/02/2012 - 10:30am

The hospital is really old and has lots of illness people and it is really noisy and dirty in the waiting room.

Peter hears a knock at the house door, as he walks to get the door he glanced in the mirror his brown short hair flicks back and his piercing blue eyes stares into the mirror. when he answers it, it was Colonel Gillian, Gillian asked "Are you ready for the doctor's Peter?"

Peter replied "Yes Gillian"

so they left to walk to the doctor's Peter lived about a ten minute walk from his house to the doctors.

They arrived at the doctor's and Peter went up to the reception, signed in the Coronal Gillian and Peter went into the waiting room and

asked Colonel Gillian "What did you do as a living"

Gillian replied. "I was in the army I was one Colonel in "world war 3 .""

Gillian asked "what do you want to do when you leave school"

Peter replied "I want to be an engineer when I leave school and go to college and university." Gillian replied "That sounds good, good luck Peter".

Gillian whispered "thats you then" they got up and walked through to the room Gillian sat next to Peter and Doctor Bains asked Peter "what can i do for you Peter"

Peter replies "I lost my auntie and uncle two months ago and I can't get over it. I always feel down and i'm never happy i'm always sad and upset about what happened and I can't get over how thore not here anymore"

Doctor Baines replied "It was like a man in the army how lost his uncle he struggled from depression"

Colonel Gillian buts in and asks "what war were you in Doctor Baines" Doctor Baines replies "World war 3 Colonel" Gillian replies "No way I was head BULLET I mean Colonel in that war"

Doctor Baines is shocked he replies "I was head doctor baines I remember you" Colonel replies in shock

"You tried to save my brothers life"

Dr Baines replies "yes it was me sorry about him passing away I tried my very best to save the lad ."

Colonel replies " Its fine don't worry there were

loads of people that died in that WASHING MA-
CHINE sorry I meant the war,, and he was probably the worst injured"

Then Peter jumps in and said "this appointment is about me not about Colonel Gillian and
Doctor Baines having chat about the war if you
two want to have a chit chat meet up somewhere
else doctor replies,

" Oh sorry Peter, i'm going renew your medication and see where it goes from there" Peter
replies,

"Ok Doctor Baines thank you for your help"
Peter and Colonel Gillian leave and walk home.

Chapter 4

The New Boy

Location: in St Patricks High School

Time: 05/02/2012 - 10:00am

The school is a nice school and is clean and they were good people there and there were bad people there at St Patricks.

David wakes up on his next day of school, gets In his school uniform and goes on he gets his breakfast. He then wakes his Mum and asks if he is getting a lift So his Mum gets up, gets dressed and tells him that hes getting a lift. He goes out to the ca, gets In and waits for his Mum.

When they arrive at school about two minutes later they park In the, car park and go into reception. The headteacher Is waiting for them to welcome them to the school. He gets a buddy who was meant to take him around the whole school for the week.

David was starting to get excited and couldn't wait untill his first period. He had history which he didn't mind but didn't really like It. He wonders how nice the teachers will be and If there strict or not. In most schools teachers are normally quite nice theres always a nice teacher and a bad teacher but the rest are quite straightforward and don't mind what you do just as long as you work.

Davids guy who was showing him around disappeared and he didn't know where to go he just stood to the side and looked for the guy who was meant to take him to classes. He couldn't see him through the crowed of people and then he saw somebody In his class In a room so he tried to get through the crowed of people and made his way to the person he thought was in the class.

David had been waiting through the whole of the summer holidays. He was very excited and sometimes he couldn't sleep at night because he was that excited and didn't know how big the school would be and what the lessons will be like or If he will make friends or not.

David even went and got the a new bag and pencils and loads more that he will need for school like a school uniform which will be quite expensive well for his family at least. He also got new schools shose and didn't know what else so he got his Mum to get all the expensive stuff because he only had what his Mum gave him and that was fifty pound.

David got worried the night before and told his Mum he didn't know if he was going to make new friends or not and his mum told him not to be silly and that he will make plenty of friends like he did at his old school. David didn't listen to what his Mum said and was still worrying but he always makes friends easily.

David before he goes to his 2nd class he starts thinking about the positives and gradually get sexcited and can't wait to start his next lessons he was so excited that he's In a new school meeting new people starting on a clean slate. He loves the new faceted nobody knows what happened at his old school they don't know about the fights he got In and the trouble he got into.

He was really excited now because nobody knows about It so he continues to not to tell anyone so nothing spreads about what he done so they wouldn't be scared of him and what he did so nobody knows about it his big secret. Then he hears the bell go and gets his back ready and gets his coat on and waits for the bell.

David hears the bell and waits to be dismissed and then he walks out to the car park and he can't see his mum so he walks home he ruffly remembers his way home and eventually got home and his mum didn't know who it was and shouted at him and he asked why she wasn't at the car park ready to pick me up I had to walk home.

Chapter 5

Getting help

Location: In Dr Baines room

Time: 06/02/2012 - 10:00am

"Louis it's nice to see you" The doctor said cheerily

"Nice too see you, now i've been having problems" replied Louis

"What sort of problems?" Dr Bains replied

"Well i've been hearing voices and its scary"

Louis saying quietly

"Next time it happens try to block it out and do not listen to them, do you have any idea who it is?" asked Dr Bains.

"Yes its my dad, he died two years ago in a fire" Louis replied

"Now I'll take some notes about this" Dr Bains told him.

"Ok Louis, I'm going to ask you some questions about these things you have been seeing, you don't need to answer the questions but it would be helpful if thats okay, now when your dad died were you there?"

"Yes" Louis said in a quiet shaky voice

"And when he talks to you what does he say¿' The doctor said weirdly

"He says things like hi how are you then it just stops" Louis replied

"Has anyone else tried to talk to you¿' Dr bains asked

"Yes but it was just all blurry, I can't remember" Louis explained

"Ok let me just go and find out what's wrong" Dr Bains explained

"Ok you have schizophrenia, now this illness can be treated, it will take time, to patients now it is a very serious illness to it will be scary but you need to try to get rid of it, Because if you don't toll anyone when its happening then it will just get worse"

"I can hear people right now" Louis shouted weirdly

"Is it anyone in particular?" asked the doctor

"No just a group of people talking, NO MAKE IT STOP"

"Blank it out, Louis ignore them think of something else. Louis these people can not hurt you the only way they can hurt you is if you let them" Dr Baines told him.

"As i just said do something to blank them out like listening to music" Dr bains replied

Louis tired as hard as he could. It just wouldn't work, nothing would! Dr Bains didn't know what to do anymore. He couldn't give him anymore information about what to do if he started to hear his dad again.

"Louis im going to give you medicine, now you have to take these two times a day or nothing will get better, you will be just letting them back in to hurt you.

"Thank you Dr baines "Louis Replied with a completely different voice from earlier"

"No bother Louis it's my job he said" He With a happier voice from earlier "if you give me two minutes i'll go and get you the prescription for the medicine. Ok Louis there is enough here to last you a month"

"Thank you so much Dr Baines!"

Louis started to leave the room but then Dr Bains spoke to his a bit more.He just couldn't stop smiling when they were both talking. Louis didn't know where to start or how to deal with what had just happened.

"Louis if you run out i'll give you a prescription for more but when you need more come back here and ask for me and, i'll give you the same medicine but if you are getting worse then i'll give you more and you'll have to come see me more often to see how your doing"

"If it gets better ill give you less medicine, you will have to come in for less check ups but if you don't hear them anymore then you can come in one last time and ill take you of the medication but if it starts again then we will have to do something else to get rid of the problem"

"Louis before you leave I need you to fill out the form for the medication and that will give you access to the medication you need "

" Thank you Louis you can now get on you way and i'll see you back here in a month or sooner if its better or worse"

"I will bye" Louise replied

Louis was going home but remembered that he had left his coat in Dr Baines room so louis had to walk all the way back to the doctors and interrupt Dr Baines when he was in with a patient

"Sorry to interrupt you Dr Baines but I forgot my coat" said Louis

"It's no bother Louis I was only just starting with my patient".

"Bye Dr Baines" "Aaaahhhhh a nice walk home"

Louis had just left the doctors and it was all fine. Louis still couldn't stop smiling, even after hours she was still smiling. Louis was quite upset, he was missing his dad. He wouldn't ever hear his voice properly again.

Chapter 6

The new school

Location:in st patricks high school

Time: 08/02/2012 - 11:00am

The path was dirty and covered in dirt there was stones and bits of gum on the floor

Peter gets up and gets dressed for school he does his normal routine - eating toast and having his orange juice, then got his shoes on and he went out the door and headed to school. He got a bit lost and didn't know which way to go at points so he followed the other kids and the lead him to the school.

David walks into his registration class and Peter saw him walked over and asked if he was new to the school and so david replied yes and that his buddy isn't very good so he had to find his way about the school and most of the time he didn't know where he was so he had to ask where his classes where and to get directed by other people.

David left his class and tries and finds his way to his next class but again he got lost and people were directing him to his next class and he just had to stop and he had to ask people but they still didn't know if they were telling the truth or not and he said to them are you sure and they start laughing and david doesn't know where to go

David saw peter walking down the corridor and asked where his music class was but peter said it was quite a bit away.

"what school did you go to before here" Peter

asked

    "a one up north why" David answered

    "dunno just asking" peter replied

    "ok weird" David answered

    "so where is this next class" david asked

    They got along like cat and milk and they didn't stop talking to each other and they didn't care about their class's and they didn't even think what to say to each other but they kept on speaking random stuff and kept on saying things but it doesn't matter what it was

    "So arc you lost then" peter asks

    "yes i am but can you show me where this class is" David

    "thats the class i've got next i can take you there if you want" David answered so they walked to their next class they didn't stop talking to each over in class and got told of a couple of times.

Chapter 7

Secrets

Location:they hang out in st patrick

Time: 08/02/2012 - 01:00pm

"Mum I'm going to David's house today it's going to be really good. We are going to play his new console and everything I cant wait to try out his new game " Drop Dead ."

"Peters coming soon we need to get ready.....come on mum hurry up.

"Ok David chill out I'll be down in a minute. Do you want me to pop out to the shops and get some treats for you boys."

"Yes please Mum."

"Bye honey I'll be back soon."

"Bye Mum."

Almost there two more streets to go I think I'll stop by the store and get some Emerge and Bon Bons."

"Oh hi Mrs Robertson " said Peter

"Hi Peter but please call me Elle, what are you doing here?"

"Oh my Mum left me some money to buy some sweets for me and David"

"I'm getting sweets too, you're going to have one big feast tonight. Oh and Peter when you get to the house tell David I'll be home soon, bye then ."

"Bye Elle .

(David looks under his bed) "So thats where my phone went. Right I've tidied: the bathroom, my bedroom, the kitchen, the game room, the study and the garden... great."

"Wow another kid getting bullied... this village is not getting any nicer, one day I hope for this village to be bully free."

"Right time for coco pops (crunch crunch crunch crunch) "

(knock knock knock) "Yay that must be Peter" David sprinted down the stairs and flung open the door.

"Hi buddy"

"Oh hi David" Peter replied

"Come up to my room I've got your favourite game "Drop Dead"

"Ok that sounds great we can also dig into these sweets I got at the shops"

"My Mum just went to the shops earlier."

"Yeah I know I met her there and she told me to tell you she's coming home with more sweets."

"Wow this console of yours is awesome I had no idea you had a mouse on the controller and you could talk to it, thats so cool."

"Yeah I know its so cool" said Peter "and I

got a 50 percent discount on it because my Uncle works at " Gum" pretty cool huh."

Chapter 8

The New Beginning

Location:The new boy joined St Patrick

Time: 12/02/2012 - 10:24am

The new boy joined the school and made good friends. He thought the school is a nice place, he thought they treat him nicely and are very kind to him.

Peter was talking to David at break time and asked how his day was going and what subjects he had. He has just got to his new school he has just gone to reception saying he is new and doesn't know his way around the school.He was a bit nervous talking to the girls at reception but he gradually got use to it. It was break and David went to the canteen, he sees Peter and he walks over to him and he asked if he was in his registration class. Peter

didn't see him there so he didn't know what to say,

"How has your day been so far" Peter randomly said,

"Good i got a bit lost earlier but i got directed in the right direction" David replied.

David saw Peter walking home so he caught up to him and they started talking to each other

"Do you wanna come over this weekend?" David

"Maybe i don't know if i'm allowed to yet" Peter replies

"Ok do you have any home work" David asks and they blaber on to each over until they see a bully picking on someone but they both have to ignore it cause they don't want any trouble. They bully stares at them and they just don't make eye contacted with him and continue walking.

Peter doesn't know what to say but he knows that his mum wants him home early today so he said.

"David ive to be home early today" he muttered out

"Okay I don't mind i'm busy to night anyway" David replied they keep on talking for a bit until they get bored and just stop talking they can see that the sun is trying to come out so they keep on walking in the spots of sunlight on the pavement and there to busy doing that that they go down the wrong road.

"Wait is this the wrong road" David asked

"Dammit yes it is we need to walk back that way" Peter shouted out they turned around and headed backwards to the road they need to go down.

"So why are you not walking with your other friends" David asked

"I don't live near them and we are all drifting apart from each over and none of us know why" Peter replied

"Thats a shame i've seen you walk about the school with them and it looked like you were all good friends" David quickly explained

"Well we were all good friends but eventually all friends need a break from each other" Peter replied

"Can we stop talking about it now I don't really like them any more" Peter asked

"Yeah ok I understand" David replied

"So do you have any brothers or sisters" Peter asked

"No im a lonely child which is kind of good what about you" David explained

"Ive got one sister who can be a pain but shes always there when I need her and she does have her benefits when she wants to use them" Peter answered it made david laugh and they went down the street that they missed.

"So what are you doing tonight " Peter asks

"Probably play the playstation cause thats like the best thing i can actually do for the rest of my night since i don't know anyone to go out and play with" David answered

"Aww thats ashame but i'm not allowed out tonight but you could add me on computer and we could play together" Peter asked

"Yeah that be fun whats game do you have" Pavid asked

"I've got Call of Ducky and my names Peter123" peter replied

"Same are we friends" David asked

"Yes we could say that we are friends" Peter answered his question

"Aw good you're my first friend" David replied they went on and on chatting for ages but they ran out of things to say. They start playing on there phones and listen to music. They go into the shops to get a drink and then they stop outside and finish their drink before they carry on walking again.

"Im so happy that were friends your a good

guy to hang out with" David told him

"I know I think we will be good friends for a while and you're also good to hang out with your a

already like a brother to me" Peter explained they're both enjoying each others company and they both dont stop laughing

"I think I might be able to come on the weekend since i've got nothing else better to do" Peter explained to him.

"that will be good we can play on my computer go to dinner and go out and you can show me about the place" Peter answered

"yes that will be well fun won't it be" peter replied in excitement

"Yeah it would be we're nearly at my house David replied

"You stay pretty close to me then cause we're nearly at my house as well "he answered

"Really thats well cool " David got a text from his mum asking where is he and just as he got the text he was at his door.

"Bye" David shouted

"Bye see you tomorrow" Peter replied.

Chapter 9

Fear

Location: in St Patricks

Time: 12/02/2012 - 12:10pm

they meet up and talk and make friends in the nice weather

and they be nice to each other and don't start fights.

David and Peter walked to school together and had fun on the way. Then they start to chat about things.

Louis see's them chatting so he wandered over to them to see what they were chatting about and wondered what they were saying .

They see Louis coming over to them so they walked him and wonders why he was coming towards them.

Louis was wanting to know how David was so peter told him and said

"he is the new boy at this school".

David said I am new at this school and peter was showing me around and being a good friend to me.

Peter introduced Lewis to David and they got all the introducing out of the way and started to chat to each other.

They now know each other so they started to chat to each other and become friends like Peter and David.

Peter asks what lesson are you at Louis and Louis did not now so his checked her timetable.

Lewis did not know so he checked his timetable

and told them the bell went for them to go back into school.

They hear the bell and go to there class's or they will be late so they ran as fast as they can and they got to class on time.

Chapter 10

Fear Of Flying

Louis and Billy become friends in the nice school called st patricks and all of them
are all happy and glad it is nice and not bad so they became really good friends.

Peter was sitting outside on the school bench missing Louis not being his friend or speaking to

him anymore. Because Louis got jealous of peter and the new boy David being best friends.
Peter wasn't very happy with Louis going away
with billy and bullying other kids. After that louis
came over to peter who was sitting on the bench
outside of the school, David came over to apolo-
gize he said "I am sorry for going away with billy
and being nasty to other kids I didn't want to but
you never left me with a choice you went away
with the new kid and left me with no one to talk
to the only person was the bully and he kind of
got me being nnasty cause what ever he went

to do I had to go with him because i had no
one to go and talk to and He was the only one
that was there for me" Peter replies "ok im sorry
to for leaving you i just did not want David to feel
all alone".

"So I went and spoke to him to see if he was
ok or not but yeah I accept your apology" Louis
replies "Thanks lets go" so they started to walk
down the road and they were talking about missing not speaking to each other and going for lunch

with each other or going to play football in the park. They were having a laugh and a joke about things shoving and pushing one another. louis says to Peter " you're my best friend and I don't want this to happen again"

Peter replied "Yeah same here i don't want us to fall out again" Louis smiled at Peter and Peter smiled at louis and they were best friends again.

Chapter 11

The second round starts

Billy was a nice kid in his last school, he would play with everyone, be nice to everyone, have fun but at the same time as he was being nice to everyone else someone was picking on Billy and giving him a very hard time. He couldn't concentrate in class, he couldn't go anywhere without getting pushed, he couldn't go home without getting beaten up, it's all because this one boy was jealous of him nice he was to other people. Billy wanted to move schools from his bully when he went to high school but he couldn't so he had to put up with his bully and other for a long time but lucky for him when he hit 6th year he was able to move and for the first time in years he was happy again.

Finally Billy got his dream to move school and become free from the bully to live a nice happy teenage life but then when he got there, he stopped to think and he thought "I want revenge on this boy for all the damage he done to me" but never did Billy want to go back to his old school so he thought to get revenge he could be a bully here and do what was done to him for years and when Billy thought this through, there was no turning back now.

So Billy went home after school that night happy,

he had a happy day but he couldn't stop thinking of his bullying plan like "does he still wanna do this?" "is this the right thing to do?" but then it just hit him, the answer in his head was yes, yes he does wanna do this, yeah he is gonna do it. The next morning at school he looks around for a kid that he could pick on. The next thing you know "PING" he spotted a kid and he looks perfect.

The next day Billy starts bullying this boy and this boy was very happy until every time he sees Billy he get very scared and tries to run away but Billys fast and always catches him.

Billy starts to slowly leave the boy alone because Billys soft side has come back and makes Billy feel really bad about bullying this boy.Billy thinks to himself for a moment "why am I taking my responsibilities out on everyone else when I can just face the fact and stand up the mess and sadness that I have caused in this world", so Billy does something about this, he goes up to this boy and tries to talk to him and say sorry. A while later the bullying stopped we thought for good but we didn't know if it would ever come back if a bully can just turn in a click.

For a little while Billy and the boy start talking and finding out stuff about each other. The boys name was Gregg and he was very nice. We started hanging out a little to make up for the damage I done to him. He told me all the damage was okay and it was healed now but I always made sure that was okay and he never once again said that he wasn't okay. He was strong, nice, caring and never once doubted me, he was an amazing friend to me and

"I guess I should cut that kid some slack for a little bit"

At the other side of the school

"I really hope Billy leaves me alone today or I might get too angry and unleash my rage and that would mean I would get into trouble and maybe get chucked out the school"

Meanwhile Billy was vandalizing and thinking about his depression.

Billy starts to wonder why he bullies people and he realises that is not cool to bully so he becomes friendly and shy.

Gregg is walking past him in the hall and drops his books, Billy dashes for them right away.

"Please dont take my books Billy"

"What you on about, I was picking them up for you I don't like bullying anymore it is horrible"

"Billy asks if they can all be friends and Gregg says yes.

In a special break Billy stands up on a bench and yells I am through with bullying.

Chapter 12

The first Attack

Location:In Gillians street

Time: 18/02/2012 - 12:00 noon

Its bright sunny day and David decides to go for a walk in the park. Davidis amazed by how hot it can actually get in Scotland because he was told it was always raining and wet. He could hear the birds tweeting, kids playing and he went, and got an ice cream from the ice cream stand. He was enjoying himself it was the hottest day in Scotland. He could see all the dogs running about chasing things he loves it, its so relaxing he goes into a shop to get an bubblegum jug which is colder than ice.

Suddenly he can hear shouting and people crying its like hell' as came he quickly rushes over and see's an old lady walking about and shouting, he went over and asked

"Why was she shoughting"she didn't reply so he quickly said

"My names David" he replied "I'm Gillian she started shouting at a dog running past she shouted "YOU CAN'T RUN THAT FAST" she keeps on ranting on and it gets worse she starts saying mean things to random people she doesn't even know them. It was really freaky David said to himself she was twitching at the same time.

Gillian is just standing by a stand and twitching and then shouting at people and david doesn't even think why. It was like she was possessed and David didn't know what to do it was beginning to scare a hearts Casual who isn't went to be scared of anything but its still scaring him. David he attempts to check if shes ok and Gillian starts talking talking to him.

"What school do you go apple" she says

"Why did you say APPLE and I go to st Patricks"

"I didn't say apple thats a new school " gillian replied

"I know but you clearly did" David moaned

David asked if she had any disabilities and she started chatting to herself. She sat down and had a drink of water and started eating sandwiches and she started acting normal for once you couldn't even tell that she was just shouting at people. Then suddenly she twitched and shouted "DAVIE TUNES" witch was really random it had nothing to do with what she was doing it looked like she was sad and lonely and a frail old lady who didn't have any friends. David felt sorry for her and went and sat next to her.

Gillian said to David

"I'm ok TREE love" Gillian replied to david

"Wait aren't you my neighbour" David said quickly

"Yes i think DOG so " Gillian mumbled out

"Thats really cool isn't" David replied with excitement

"Yes that is WOOF quite cool" Gillian said sarcastically.   Gillian gets up and twitches but doesn't say anything and keeps on walking, David gets up and follows her and she starts shouting at people saying a bunch of random stuff. Some of it I laughed at because it was quite funny. She kept on turning around and shouting at people behind him. David started running and he caught up to Gillian.

David starts talking to Gillian and he asked if she works for a living. She doesn't reply she still walking very fast foward and she trips on rocks a couple of times and david tells her to slow down and that he won't hurt her she gradually slows down and walks normally and David asks why was she walking so fast and she didn't know why she said that she just felt like it for no reason

David was starting to annoy her but she was out of breath so david and gillian go sit down on a park bench. but then David saw a girl walking.

Gillian started staring at the girl that was walking fast david thought to himself that she was going to "TSUNAMI"she shouted at her david was so embarrassed that he walked away for a bit and then david decided to come back. He didn't know what to say he was that embarrassed he just sat there next to her. David just sat there thinking what to do because it was just do embarrassing for him.

"Why did you say that" david asked her

"Say what" Gillian replied

"Calling that girl a tsunami" David said

"I don't know" Gillian said confusingly

"Well" david said you have to be nice be to other people. You have to respect other members of the public including animals and other things you don't see people walking about, shouting at other people for no reason. If I saw somebody doing that I would think that they're a bad person and would try and ignore them and carry on with my day. You look like a nice lady and I try and see through the bad parts of people.

"Sorry well ok mr big boots" Gillian replied

"See thats what i mean you shouldn't do that to people.

"Look I have tourettes" Gillian told him

"Thats why you were being really weird, well strange shouting at all them people for no reason"

"Yes thats why, RED STICK I developed them after World War 3 just after KFC IS BAD but I Can't CATFIGHT control them like that. Gillian replied

"Ok how old were you when you were in WW3" david asked

"I dont know now it was BOBCAT a long time ago" Gillian Muttered out

"What was it like" David asked

"I dont want to DUCK talk about it" Gillian said loudly

"Ok i understand" David replied.

"I'm sorry for have a go at you i have just been

taught that its not right to shout at other people like that." david replied syimpicfeticly

"I know its ok it allways GOLF BALL happens and I get AIRPLANE use to it after a while" david sits and chats with her until he had to go home he fought it was nice to learn a bit about the war and one of his neighbours who is a nice old lady who nobody understood until today where david finally understand her and why she starts shouting randomly at people who she doesn't know and the truth is that he felt sorry for her.   f

Chapter 13

Out Of Sight Out Of Mind

Location:In St Patricks high school

Time: 18/02/2012 - 10:ooam

Louis needed a friend because he had fallen out with Peter and Gregg and David so instead of going to make friends with them he goes and talks to the bully. Louis and Billy become good friends and they are together quite a lot of the day.

Billy has always been a bully and just because he got a new friend doesnt mean hes gonna stop bullying, so Louis agrees to bully people with Billy and together they are the new school bullies and are going to pick on everyone and Bill is going to teach Louis how to bully!

Louis never thought to find himself in a position where he bullies people but then he does, and he has a good feeling about it. Louis is never been classed as a bully unless it was a joke but this time its not a joke, its real and Louis is a bully, the new bully of the school.

Louis doesn't think theres any point in being friends with Peter so he goes to tell Peter the news when she finds Peter with David which makes her upset. Nothings holding Louis back from telling the news though, so when he got to Peter he was laughing and he was really happy. Louis tells Peter the disturbing news and Peter all of a sudden turn very angry and depressed.

The group of children have no contact for weeks

apart from Billy and louis are always together.

Louis tries to talk to Peter but he doesn't wanna talk to him so she tries the others but nobody's talking. Eventually Peter, David and Gregg start talking again but nobody's talking to Louis because the feel like they have been betrayed by him and if they feel that way they don't need to talk to him.

Chapter 14

The Start Of Something

Location:In school grounds

Time: 21/02/2012 - 11:00am

Louis and Peter are starting to drift apart and Louis started to get jealous so he decided to start talking to the bully. Billy is one of the worst bullies at St Patricks. Billy was the type of person to go to school wearing tracksuits with weird looking trainers. Billy was sixteen years old. He was six foot tall and has blue eyes and brown short hair. Billy likes all kind of music so some music he listens to was quite weird. Billy had been bullying for four years and if Louis started to bully, it could get a whole lot worse.

Louis started to get jealous and annoyed of when Peter meets David and starts to hang around with him more than Louis, so Louis decided to go and hang with the Billy the bully for a bit. Louis then started to get kind of close to the bully since Louis and Peter weren't talking very much any more.

Louis and Billy eventually start to get on. Billy then starts to get Louis involved in what he does, bullying, little by little. Louis and Billy weren't that close that you could call them "friends" just yet. As the days past they got a bit closer each day. Louis didn't give much thought about Peter and David becoming friends because Louis thinks that its better as friends with Billy not Peter.

As the days and hours went past they started to hang out more and more each day. Louis started enjoying what he was doing with Billy. Billy and Louis had new plans and ideas each day of with prank or jokes to play on everyone. I've not actually said but Louis isn't bullying just yet. Louis doesn't have the guts in him just yet. Billy has tried to persuade Louis to try with him just once but Louis isn't taking any of it, not just yet.... anyway.

Now Louis and Billy are at the stage where you can start calling them "friends". They started to hang out after school, and they actually started to have a good time together. They aren't at the point where they are really close, not just yet because they only met about a week ago. Billy got a bit annoyed at Louis for not joining him. Billy started to shout at Louis,

Billy started to say to Louis "why don't you just try it, its fun... is it because you're scared?.... haha scaredy cat, scaredy cat"

"I'm not a scaredy cat I just don't want to do

it, I might do it soon just to see what its like....
maybe, I'm not saying I will do it though!" replied
Louis in an annoyed voice.

" Aye aye whatever you say, haha" shouting at
Louis

For the next few minutes it was an awkward
silence between Louis and Billy. Billy wanted to
apologise what saying what he said but he couldn't
say anything. Billy couldn't figure it out, why?,
Why wont he do it? Billy didn't ask Louis why
he would do it, he just left bit and said he would
meet him tomorrow at school.

The thing that happened between Louis and
Billy the other night was out of sight and out of
mind. Louis decided to not start and do anything
apart from talk to Billy. Louis was walking into
the hall to meet Billy at St Patricks and seen Peter
and David laughing and having fun and all Louis
could think about was when him and Peter youst
to laugh and have so much fun but all of that
was destroyed. Billy seen Louis look at Peter and
David. Billy did ask if Louis was okay but Louis

just said he was fine, nothing else apart from fine. Louis just ignored it and got on with the day. Louis and Billy started to have a good laugh with each other and they were starting to get really close as friends. They were starting to become something near best friends. Louis was wanting to try do some things with Billy now just to try it, not to continue on bullying for the rest of the years but he doesn't really know what he wants to do just yet.

Louis and Billy are now beginning to be so close just like Best Friends, now Louis wasn't giving a Second thought about Peter and David. They were completely out of the picture now. Louis officially now had a new best friend. Louise and BIlly are completely different, no one would've thought they would of become friends. Louis was now definitely giving it a second thought about what Billy said earlier on, about how he should try it. Louis couldn't stop thinking about it even when he was in classes. Louis was at home and he still couldn't get it off his mind. Louis went to sleep and he never thought about it until he saw Billy the next day.

Louis was all ready for school this day and he never thought about it once. He was at school and he looked at Billy and started to panic for no reason at all. He started to think if he wanted to do it but he couldn't make up his mind. He wants to do it but he doesn't at the same time, he doesn't want to let Billy down to say he won't do it. Louise doesn't say anything to Billy at the start because he's thinking about if he should join him today or not. Billy could tell something was up but he didn't mention anything. Louis started to swear and feel dizzy with all the pressure he thinks he is on.

Billy didn't know what to say so he said the first thing that came into his mind "so... em... Louis do want to join me? you don't have to if you dont want to"

Louis tried so hard not to mumble the answer with his shaky voice "em....em...... I sup....posse I could just for today maybe, it...... could be fun"

"Oh My God, are you being serious about this, I didn't think you would ever say you would!" replied Billy

"em....em yeah I could just for to..today though" Louis saying in his mumbling voice

Billy was starting to see something was up because Louis was shaking, sweating and he was swaying side to side a little bit.

"Louis are you okay you look a bit......weird, not like in a bad way or anything I mean you're sweatin mumbling and all sorts today, are you okay Louis?"

Louis could barely speak.

"yes.....yes, Im......im fine, i think haha" replied Louis

Louis and Billy got to work on their new plan for bullying someone. when they were both planning it Louis started to forget about it and not feel so pressured. Louis and Billy were having some fun actually. It was soon becoming to that time they became best friends.

Billy and Louis have a big argument and they

might have a chance at splitting up. None of them want to split up but sometimes we don't get to decide. Billy and Louis have an argument because Louis misses Peter and the rest of them and he doesnt wanna bully people anymore so she wants to make things right with Peter, Gregg and David.

Billy and Louis take a break from each other so they can try and make things right with their other friends. They think its best if they stay away from each other for now until they make things right.

Chapter 15

One On One

Louis was all alone and feeling lonely and sad in the playground with no friends
to play with and to have fun with so he was really sad and scared of Billy the bully
because he picks on any one to hurt them and makes them sad and lonely is something you don't

want and Louis was upset and scared in the the playground.

Billy walked up to him and picked on him and calling him names and hitting him really hard

and maked him cry and be scared to come back to school, but he and bullied Louis

and Billy found it funny and fun to bully people Louis was really upset and covered in bruises and scratches all over his body.

Billy was trying to make him feel bad but Louis started getting bullied and getting upset because of Billy.

Louis was feeling very upset, unhappy and unwanted at his school and no one wanted to play with him so he feels really upset and unwanted by his friends.

Louis was wanting to see his friend but they were playing with the new boy who joined the school and they wanted to make him feel safe and wanted at that school but Louis was jealous of him.

Louis went to the doctors because he had depression and was not happy and was really sad and jealous of the new boy called David and Louis was depression of him and getting bullied by Billy

Louis was thinking about it, he should go to get help but he does not go and see him he leaves it.

His friends where just hanging around with the new boy and Billy came back and bullied him again.

Billy starts bullying Louis again Billy comes back and bullied him again and Louis got really sad again and got upset because of Billy the bully and got angry .

Louis got angry and stormed away from Billy and was really angry and upset at Billy and his friends.

Chapter 16

One Moment

Location:at the school

Time: 23/02/2012 - 01:05pm

Peter remembered when he found out about his auntie and uncle had died that night Peter felt terrible and ever since that night Peter had been depressed. Peter thought to himself why was it that them that died that night why could it not of been another person Auntie and Uncle. Peter loved his

Auntie and Uncle he used to go and visit them on a Friday and Peters Auntie used to make his favourite sausage, beans, and mash potatoes and then he went and played football and basketball in the back garden, then they came in and put a movie on and Peters Auntie would bring through some crisps and sweets. Peter kept on going on about why he always feels sad and upset.

Peter then he gets really upset and he can't stop thinking about it, how he felt when his Mum told him that they had passed away. Peter was gutted, Peter kept on going on about when he used to go round on a Friday after school and play darts but he couldn't anymore because they were not here for him to do that.

Chapter 17

Could It Be The End?

Location: St Patricks High School

Time: 26/02/2012 - 10:00am

Louis and Billy were hanging out at the park when all of a sudden they seen some swans floating across the lake ever so delicately so they decide to run to the near by burger van and ask for some burger buns to feed the swans, when they return to the lake the swans were still swimming along without a care in the world.

"Do you like this park Lewis asked Billy and he replied yes I used to come here as a child with my parents, "

"who is that over there on the swing, is that David and who is that with him"?

"Louis It looks like?" Peter replied Louis

"Lets go" whispered Billy.

Louis stays quiet and walks slowly behind Billy

"Whats wrong with you Louis you look sad"

"Admits that he is sad and that he has mucked up breaking away from Peter"

"why do you miss him said Billy"

"Because he is my mate and nothing changes that"

"Haha he hates you now"

Billy starts to moan and groan at Louis saying you shouldn't be friends with that ignoramus"

"Shut up Billy you "

"Dont fall out with me like you did with little

lover boy"

"Shut up you idiot"

"Just leave "

Louis grabs his belongings and storms away huffing and puffing.

"I never should have trusted that twat I hate him I never should have let Peter go he said to himself.

In Billy's room he starts to cry

"Why do I always muck things up between me and my friends"

Billies parents hear Billy scream and shout, they say nothing because they want it all out off him but then they hear a smash.

"Billy what on earth are you doing up here on the floor"

She then discovers his smashed tv and screams even more.

"You are in big trouble mister you are grounded for a month.

Billy keeps raging.

"Shut up, you can't tell me what to do, I don't

care if you say you can, you are not the boss of me go away.

Chapter 18

Changes

Louis is walking to school and sees Peter walking to school with the the kid David and he doesn't like the new kid David so he walks over and starts talking to Peter to try and stop the attention going to David but david notices what he is doing and tells peter later. Louis gets really jealous and breaks off the friendship.

Louis is jealous so he makes new friends with the bully and leaves Peter alone. He is that jealous that that he might break away from her group of friends. Louis starts hanging out with the bully at break time and lunch time and Peter notices that she is hanging out with the bully.

Louis starts the help the bully do what he does best bully and get up to mischief and he is enjoying it. He bullies kids for their lunch money and push people. Peter Gregg and David all see him doing it and he looks like she is loving it and keeps on doing it for her enjoyment and doesn't stop doing it.

They love to bully other people that they don't like and people that bullied Louis before he was friends with the bully were all bullied they were pushed, punched, hair was pulled and do whatever they wanted to do to them and they both love doing it especially when they make people cry. Its got that bad that when they walked down the corridor every one moves to the over side.

Chapter 19

The Crazy Mind

Location: gillians house

Time: 28/02/2012 - 4

One day David was bored so he asked if he could go see Gillian his Mum let him so he went over and knocked on her door but Gillian forgot who he was and she asked who he was and David replied saying "David from the park" and she still remembered who he was so she let him in for a cup of juice.

"What juice do you want David" Gillian asked politely

"The lemon one please" David replied David's favourite, one he always gets it when hes there.but there is another one that he loves but she normally doesn't have it cause its her favourite one as well but David does get it now and then if hes nice or not but its normally a treat when he does get it.

"There you go David here's a nice drink for you" Gillian said but the Gillian dropped the glass and started throwing things like books and sticks and anything that she could grab in and through and then she started calling him fat and useless and all sorts of things but it has been the worst of them yet, Davids adrenaline was trying to kick in but he had to keep it back because we will do .what he does to other casuals. David didn't know what to do because he can't hit a old lady.

Gillian saw what he was doing so she pinned him up against the wall david didn't know what to do because if he just kit her he hit her she could die or get put in hospital and he could get arrested but she started suffocating him so he pushed her on to the sofa and she fell backwards and landed on the sofa nicely without hurting herself so David started shouting

"stop Stop what are you doing its david" he shouted at the top of his voice.

"leave me alone stop it what's wrong with you" David shouted.

David sat down and when he looked up he saw a gun pointed at him he panicked and jumped over and hid behind the sofa and hid he was thinking about calling the police but then she would get arrested and sent to prison or a care home which wouldn't be fair. David peeked around the sofa and saw that she had put the gun down he sat there for a bit longer just incase she shot him so he waited about ten minutes before he got up and asked her if she was ok.

She stared at him and said who are you David was speechless he was acting like she was possessed by the Devil and he didn't know what to say she looked so evil he told her to calm down and take a seat so she listened and she sat down but didn't stop staring at him for about five minutes and about five minutes after that she was acting normal and like nothing had happened which was really creepy but David was still speechless. He was sat there frozen sold for about five minutes and then david started to move again he was petrified he had his neighbour point a gun at him

so David looked at the clock and saw that he had to go home. He offered to tidying her room but she said that it was ok and that he should just go home but he stayed and did some tidying up for her because she couldn't do it because of her arm it would of hurt her a lot to do all of it. I looked at the time it was 10:00 I rushed home as fast as I could which was ok because I lived right next door I shouted "bye" as he ran.

David didn't tell his mum anything about what happened that night he felt like she would call the cops on her so he had to leave it. But every time he looks out the window he remembers that moment it was one of the scariest moments of his life so he just stayed away from her for quite a bit before he went back. He had to recover from that event that happened. He didn't know what to do he didn't want to go back over but he had to to see if she was alright but he left it for a bit because he didn't want her to do it again.

2 weeks later he looked out the window and Gillian was right there staring right at him.

David imagined her lifting up her gun at him and firing at him... quickly he ducked after, he stood up again Gillian was thinking what is he doing he looks like a space hopper turns out she was just waving. david immediately shut the curtains and ran off.

Chapter 20

The colonel's houses

```
Location:in Gillians house

Time: 28/02/2012 - 06:20pm
```

David gets an invite from his neighbour to go for dinner at her house. He doesn't know why she always invites him over he hasn't even got to know her that well but he has a think about it. He goes upstairs and goes on his console and he keeps on dying on dread run so he goes of it and then he goes and knocks on Gillian's door.

David says I'll come for dinner if you want gillian. He goes in and takes a seat and asks what's for dinner and she says pasta with sausage in it David asks how her day has been and she tells him how lonely she was that day and that she missed her husband that died.

We have pasta with sausage in it for tea she told David.

"That sounds quite nice" David replied

"It verry nice I Always use to eat it all the time when I got back from the war" Gillian told him

"Bet you use love to eat it, it sounds amazing" David replied

"It was and then I use to get ice cream and brownies and have a cup of hot chocolate" gillian explained to David.

"what type of sausage is it" David asked

"Smoked sausage" she answered

"I love that one I use to get it with chips and tomato ketchup it was amazing "David told her

"I know I use to have, that when I was a little girl it was my favourite thing to eat" Gillian answered

they go on sharing their childhood memories.

"I better lay the table" Gillian explained

"I could help you if you want" David replied

"Its ok you came over to my house so I do the work" she answered back

"If you're sure I can I help if you want me to" David replied

"No you just sit back and relax" Gillian told him. So david sat back and put his feet up and did what she told him to do.

"What would you like to drink" david heard Gillian asking

"That lemon one please" David asked

"I will check if I have any more of that one left" Gillian answered

"Ok" David replied,

"Ive got some" Gillian shouted

"Yes thats my favorite " david answered

"I know it is I have been running out of it " Gillain shouted david took a drink and lent back and put his feet up again.

David got up and went and sat at the table with Gillian he asked her how long till dinner and she said it was ready so he went and got his dinner and sat down at the dinner table and tuck in to his dinner he fell in love with it, it was his favorite dinner now he loved it that much.

David had seconds and thirds he loved it that much and then he asked what was for dessert and she replied that they were having ice cream and brownies.

Gillian gets up and goes and gets the brownies from out the oven and then asks david what ice cream flavour he would like on his brownies he says mint and she says that she just has enough

for both of them she quickly gives him his brownie while its hot because its better when its hot just like cakes and pies.

David finishes his dessert and goes and does the washing up for Gillian and then he sits down and finishes his drink and thanked Gillian for tea and said his goodbyes and went home when he went home and told his mum everything that they did there. His mum liked it and found it interesting and she said that he can go over when ever he wants to.

Chapter 21

What To Expect

```
Location:Airport

Time: 02/03/2012 - 01:00pm
```

Uncle Bill was coming from Himalayas to see Gregg his nephew who he has never seemed to spend lots of time with him and see what he what to do with his uncle for the day.

Uncle Bill arrived and went to see Gregg at his house and see what he has done all these years, until now he said I have be good and I have to work hard at school. "I could not wait to see you for one day or more".

Gregg and Uncle Bill spent lots of time together, they talked and went to lots of places when he came over to see him and take Gregg out for an ice cream and to a talk about life and what he has done all these days.

Uncle Bill tells Gregg what he has been up to all these years and he said that he

was at Himalayas

all these years and cames to see him for a couple of days then he was going home and he said lets go out for a walk so Gregg and Uncle Bill went out for a walk.

Gregg and Uncle Bill go out for a ice cream they pick their favorite ice cream

and they pick the same kind of ice cream and Gregg said you like that flavor of ice cream and

they went home.

On there way back home they talk about their hobbies and they have some in coming but not a lot in coming so they said we have some but not a lot of thing in coming and the same hobbies so they talked about other things and what they have done all these years.

They are a bit of the same not a lot the same but they have the same power and

they have that incoming they are incoming for some but they share the same power and problems so they talked about the day today.

Uncle Bill is going to teach Gregg how to work his powers and what it is and how it works and what it does to help him and others and see what it can do.

Gregg goes and helps his friends by heals them with Uncle Bill and he saves his friends with his power and learned how to heal others thanks to Uncle Bill...

Chapter 22

The Different Sounds

```
Location:Airport

Time: 03/03/2012 - 02:35pm
```

"I cant wait to see my Uncle Bill I've never seen him before I wonders what he looks like" "He probably is quite old and has grey hair from what I have heard he went to the himalayas quite extravagant"

"Yes it is wonderful i have so many questions to ask him like what was it like, who did you meet, how did you fell"

"Yes yes I am sure you do replied his Dad"

"Do you think he got us presents "

"it is a possibility you go on in I will wait in the car "

"Ohh where is he I can't find him anywhere I need to find him, before he thinks we forgot to pick him up",

as Uncle Bill was sitting on the plane.

"I cant wait to touch down said Uncle Bill"

"Where is he i have to find him i want to meet him"

"Finally I have landed that plane ride was absolutely horrendous now in see why some planes include barf bags", "His plane has finally arrived I can finally meet Gregg this will be great"

"Where is that little kid i have missed him",

"Maybe he has forgot to come for me but then again I have not seen him in fourteen years, I won't have a clue what he looks like and I don't want to use magic in a public place people will start to get suspicious and thats the last thing I Want"

"I Will just have to find him by patrolling the area"

"I need to find him but he might have missed the flight what if he has this is a tragedy, ok Gregg calm down everything will be fine"

all I want is to meet him",

"I will have to search for him",

" What was that noise did you hear that to young man"

"Yes but nobody else seemed to lets ask someone"

"Wait are you Gregg simpson collins boy"

"way wait a minute are you Bill, Bill Anderson"

"Yes i am its nice to finally meet you i have dying for this day to come"

"As have I"

"Lets go, Dads waiting in the car"

"Uncle Bill how did you know it was me?"

"I heard the magic bells"

"Do you belive in magic Uncle Bill"

"If you believe in something enough it is possible in my opinion"

There is something i haven't told my parents that i will tell you if you promise not to tell them"

"I promise"

"I can do magic"

"I should hope so because i can do magic to but we will talk about it later"

" ok"

" oh and by the way Uncle Bill mum is throwing a welcome home party.

" Well i appreciate it your Mother was always there for me.

"I am so glad that your home Uncle Bill This will be great fun"

"Same here buddy we will have a great time"

" Good to see you Bill its been awhile"

"Same to you old friend how have you been doing"

"Just working what about you"

"Studying religion"

Chapter 23

Flaws

Location:in gregs house

Time: 06/03/2012 - 07:30pm

As the three men pull up to the house they seem to notice a lot of rucas and lights on in every other house in the street but not in theres so Bill automatically presumes that the party was a lie but when they open the car door fireworks flee from the back garden so Bill gets a tingly feeling and suddenly the lights come on and the banners are revealed saying welcome home Bill.

"Do you like it Uncle Bill it was all my idea" said Gregg.

"Thanks kid."

" Before we go in there I have to say this is great and all but I have to say I don't like it"

Greggs face starts to weep but Uncle Bill said,

"I dont like it because I love it"

suddenly Greg's face light up and he said,

"Thanks Uncle Bill it really means a lot to me so thats why I was so upset when you said that you didn't like it."

"Well I am sorry kid I was just messing with you"

"The best adventure I had whilst away in the beautiful himalaya mountains was when I came across a grand ancient temple on the side of the mountain, I first discovered it by helicopter but that was a boring way to get into it so I abseiled down the mountain and I had to break my way into this temple because the doors were frozen shut, once inside i made it past several booby traps such as rapid arrows, a great sized boulder and a pit of snakes, after all these tests he made it to the gold room and thats how I struck it rich"

Gregg starts to tell Uncle Bill that he was telling them about adventures not how he got some cash.

"Oh sorry Gregg any way back to the story"

Uncle Bill thanks everyone for the party and cuts the cake happily with some of the cream dropping of the side and jam running from the middle, everybodies face lit up and sixteen plates flew towards Uncle Bill.

"Yes don't worry everybody will get a bit and we will all enjoy it"

"I loved the party tonight and this was a great experience to remind me from my old life back here but I will have to leave"

"No dont leave stay here" said Gregg

"Uncle Bill explains that he will have to leave to miss the horrendous traffic on the motorway when..."

"Nonsense" said susan "You can stay here tonight

or for the next few days until you settle back in this town.

Uncle Bill starts to show his gratitude.

"Thank you Susan you were always there for me even as a child you were always there"

"I suppose it would be nice to have some company on the first or so nights"

With no hesitation whatsoever Uncle Bill agrees to stay at Gregg's house.

The two walked off.

Chapter 24

Flaws

Location:in gregs house

Time: 09/03/2012 - 02:04pm

Uncle Bill does not know whether he should tell Gregg about his supernatural powers incase he does not want to use them and if it wrecks his life then he will be the one to blame.

Uncle Bill wonders whether to tell Gregg how to use his powers. For future life reasons incase he needs to help somebody but Uncle Bill thinks he might use them wrong and end up getting into trouble

Gregg is very upset and depressed because he is struggling to learn how to use his powers and can not get the way to use them right and if he can't get them right then he will do something terribly wrong.

Bill thinks he should tell Gregg how to use them because he is worried he is going to hurt somebody or damage something then will have to pay a fine for.

Bill explains to Gregg that he has powers as well even though Gregg knows about his own powers but does not know how to use them when Uncle Bill does know how to use them.

"Greg I have something to tell you. I have supernatural powers"

"Well I Have powers as well"

"Well greg maybe I Could show you how to use them"

"Yes that would be great if its not to much

hasell"

"Uncle Bill can you show me what you know"

"Yeah i don't see why not Gregg"

after half an hour Gregg started to practice he was struggling

Uncle Bill can I show you what I already know yeah sure".

After a wee while of Gregg showing Uncle Bill what he knows Uncle Bill tells Gregg that is nothing compare to what he knows and tells Gregg he needs to learn more.

"Gregg why are you getting so annoyed and agitated "

"Because you said that was nothing and it was rubbish"

"I didn't say that I just said you need more practice "

"Well would you help me practice controlling it and get better"

"yes but you've got to promise not to get annoyed ok".

"now calm down Gregg or I will not teach you

because I can not teach you if your getting angry
all the time because you will just not learn".

Chapter 25

Noon

Location:gregs house

Time: 08/03/2012 - 12:07 noon

Uncle Bill has a very strange feeling inside and is not sure if Gregg knows why only the two of them heard the magic noise so Uncle Bill decides to tell him.

"Gregg there is something i need to tell you about what happened at the airport"

"What is Uncle Bill"

"Do you know why only the two of us could hear the magical sound when we walked past each other"

The tension builds up and Gregg said.

"Yes i know why, its all because of magic and i can see GHOSTS Uncle Bill, thats right GHOSTS and if you don't believe me i will show you look Uncle Bill look."

"Thats enough Gregg i believe you i can see them as well."

"So that means we are special Uncle Bill are we freaks to have this power."

"No son we are just unique compared to others in this world."

"Can you show me more Uncle Bill i really wao earn more like how to control it."

perhaps i can train you but you will have to wait a few weeks until i settle back to my old lifestyle."

Later that night in Greggs bed room.

"Yes, Yes, Yes, Yes, Yes i am going to learn

more about my magic yahoo i am so excited"

Susan, Greg's mother appears from the living
room

"Are you alright my little man i heard you
shouting some outrages rucas about learning magic
or something like that"

"oh a yes mum i was just playing with my toys
mum i hope i didn't disrupt your x factor viewing"

"Haha very funny you little magician"

"Haha great banter mum you always crack me
up"

"You're not an egg Gregg just be a little bit
quieter"

"Ok mum"

Uncle Bill walks to Greg's house and goes up
stairs into Greg's room.

"Hey kid how are you doing i got you a chocolate bar"

Gregg takes the chocolate bar and snaps it in
half generously and gives half of it to his Uncle
Bill

"Thanks kid i was thinking how about we take

a walk in the park together"

"which park do you mean"

"Brown wood park said Uncle Bill"

"Thats to near the hospital, my friends live in the hospital because they have a mental illness"

"why don't we try to help them"

"If we are going to save them we need to work together and come up with a plan"

Uncle Bill explains.

"Why don't you be in charge of this one because you know thee boys better than i do"

Greg replied

"Ok i will do for my friends and together we will save them"

Uncle Bill tries himself first because he tells Gregg he might not be ready to perform magic on humans and it might only make it worse for his friends." With a flick of a wrist and in a flash you will feel better and in a trance"

" Gregg asks is it working Uncle Bill is it working"

Uncle Bill falls back and has failed to heal Greggs

two best friends.

"Please Uncle Bill Try one more time i think we can do it if you let me try it to"

"Uncle Bill if you don't try again my friends will be horrible there whole lives and i need friends Uncle Bill i really love these guys"

"Icant i will fail i have no power left I have to wait to get my energy back"

"Well try to regain your powers faster demanded Gregg"

"I will try for you my boy"

They waited for thirty minutes to regain Uncle Bill and finally when he had his powers charged up again he said.

"I dont want to do it again Gregg it will just be harder for your friends to cope with and i dont want to mess them up any more it is far too dangerous to attempt, and i can't live with knowing that i hurt two of my wonderful nephews best friends"

Whilst crying he starts to tell his Uncle Bill

"that he has spoken to them and they are willing to take the risk so why will you not help us or better still why will you not let me try to cure my friends because if you don't try to help them i will"

Uncle Bill Includes Gregg into this final attempt and they both try to heal Greggs best friends

"Lets do this Uncle Bill i have faith in us"

"So do i but all my faith is in you said Uncle Bill"

The two magic men clenched eachothers hands and started to say With a flick of a wrist and in a flash you will feel better and in a trance repeatedly until the two boys starts to rise up and glow with purple dust, and as they land perfect on the ground the two boys felt great.

Peter and lois start to cry a river of tears of joy and start running around jumping and shouting and Gregg said to Uncle Bill

"I have never seen them so happy in seven years and i am so glad they are cured"

Gregg walks up to a blank wall and stares deeply into it, Uncle Bill knows right away what he is doing and walks over to see what he can see and can see his parents, Uncle Bill's parents talking to Greg telling him what a great man his Uncle is.

The two walked off.

so that

Chapter 26

Open time

Location: Peter and Rachel in the living room

Time: 12:45pm

Peter was in the house himself and he is upset about why he was depressed he can't stop getting bad thoughts in his head then his sister Rachael rushes in and comes to cheer peter up so rachel came and sat next to peter and ask him what he is up to what he wants to do Peter said "nothing really"

Rachael replies.

"We have to do something, hows about we take the dog for a walk"

Peter replies

"Yes why not I will got put the dog on the lead" Rachel replied

"Yeah that sounds good"

they left the house and went to the park and Peter brought a ball to play catch and to chuck the ball for the dog on the way Rachel made a few jokes like

"Roses are red.

Your blood is too.

You look like a monkey

And belong in a zoo.

Do not worry,

I'll be there too.

Not in the cage,

But laughing at you".

Peter replies in laughter "hahahahaha very funny you've made my day now lets get back tea will be ready soon"

Rachael replies "yeah sounds good we will play with the dog on the way down they play on the way to the house with the dog they get in the house and sit on the couch then there mum and dad came in and asked what they have been up to they answer

"We took the dog on a walk"

Peter asks mum and dad what they were up to and mum replied

"I am away to make the dinner with Rachel"

Dad says to Peter

"Do you want to go and play darts up stairs"

Peter replies "yeah sounds good to me"

So they went up and played darts then came back down to have dinner.

Chapter 27

About Time

```
Location: gillians house

Time: 10/03/2012 - 09:10pm
```

(phone rings, phone rings)"hello this is David speaking.",

"Oh hi BIGHEAD.", I was wondering if you maybe want to DRIVE, sorry come and visit for WEE WEE sorry what i meant to say was tea and snacks and i've got your favorite because you are a FAT SLOB, sorry i mean kind BOBBLES I mean person.", He said Nervously

"Erm thanks Gillian i'll see you soon then bye." Louis Said uncomfortably

"Oh by the way David i'm sorry i messed up the phone call i really did try" He said with a sad face on the other line

"Thats ok Gillian bye." Louis replied weirdly

"Bye MANGLE BOB, I mean David"

"Bye Gillian."

The next morning David went over to Gillians house. "CREEK." David opened the door carefully incase she threw something at him but today she seemed more relaxed almost as if she sort of knew she had company today and calmed down.

"Now David why don't you sit down and have ROPUGNIF i mean something to eat and drink."

"Oh those biscuits look good."

"Thanks I made them myself, I call them the DROOPS I mean Colonels Crackers."

"Mmm there delish how do you make them my secret. If you want some more you will have to come over and get them.",

"Ok now do you want to hear some stories?"

"Yeah tell me about the training."

"well David, if you ever want to join the army you're going to have to get past the training course."

"I could pass it easy."

"Ok then wait till you hear this. First you have to run round a of a mile field 10 times then crawl under 50m of barbed wire to simulate the trenches you then have to swim through a pool of mud then bench press 250, 25 times then hold your breath for 10 minutes, every minute GOODS sorry I mean you're allowed a breath for RAGGY BONGS I sorry what I meant, two seconds.

"Anyway the worst thing for me was the climbing test."

"Why what happened there"

"Well you had to climb a 150ft wall. Everybody else was fine but me."

"Well what happened to me was two steps up the wall the ropes broke up the top end broke i jumped down with 2 ton cables landing on my right arm."

"Wow thats a big scar." He replied with his eyes wide open

" Yep two foot long she is and what a belter too" Said with a smile on his face

"Did it hurt" asked david

"Did they take good care of you" Asked Gillian

"Did you have to go to hospital" Louis asking All Questions

"Yes it hurt for a start" Said with a screwed up face

"But the colonel didn't really care he just shouted medic and walked of."

"The thing that really bums me out is GO-RILLA DONG oops I meant to say that they just gave me something to ease the pain, a bandage and went back to the stand by room HOPING sorry i get nervous and these things PLIP out I mean they didn't even clean it they just walked off and left me to recover."

"wow that was a lot to take in, my goodness look at the time i'm sorry Gillian but i've got to go home its 7:00 time for my tea."

"Bye Gillian."

"Bye DAVID FLOPPY FACE."

Chapter 28

The Delivery

Location: in the the school

Time: 12/03/2012 - 3:00pm

"Hey Gillian I have somthing to ask you, ...
do you want to be best friends?"

"Why of course, I would love to be best friends
and TROTTER eh neighbours."

"Yay"

"How is your family by the way?"

"Oh my CTV, family sorry yeah my family is fine considering half of them died in the War. I can show you my family tree if you like."

"Ok that would be cool."

"Ah here's the old thing, ... theres me, theres my brother, there my mum, and theres my dad."

"Wow your dad was a High General, ...Your Mum was in the black cops, ...and your brother was a dogfighter."

"I love having young people around to my house that I can tell my stories to, someone that will actually listen to my stories. Its quite fun actually."

"Oh I have to go now bye bye see you tomorrow my mum will be worried about me and have to go to my Grans today anyway I'll see you tomorrow, my gran is going to teach me how to use cheats on "Death run "

Chapter 29

Time Travel

```
Location:in gregs house

Time: 13/03/2012 - 11:45am
```

"This is very hard uncle bill I don't think I can do these things" Uncle Bill forms his hands together and opens them there is a fire ball in his hands

"Wow" exclaimed Gregg

"You can not do this if it were to get in the

wrong hands there would be mass destruction"

"Ok" said gregg in a disappointed voice.

"You need to push very hard do not stop I certainly will not stop pushing you"

"This is hard" said Gregg

"Do you want to learn this or not" Uncle Bill shouted

"Of course I do" Gregg shouted back

"Ok, then push harder"

"Look I can not do this, it's to difficult and complicated" moaned Gregg

"Well you have to try harder don't you"

"Never ever am I going to do this"

"Yes you will" said Uncle Bill

"No I won't"

"Fine then if you stand there saying I can't do this you will never do it"

"Fine then I will give it some more goes"

"Alright then clap your hands together and rub thw

em together and push then open your hands and look down close your eyes now open your eyes can you see the ghosts yet?"

"No" said Gregg in an exasperated voice.

"Right this is the last time I'm doing it"

"Massive push Gregg" exclaimed Uncle Bill "Right so do what I told you clap your hands together rub them close your eyes open them look down look up can you see them"

"Yes yes I can see them I can now see animals also this is so cool oh my, Rover"

" Who is rover" "my old boxer dog he died last year I am so happy come here boy" Gregg said in a loving voice "thank you Uncle Bill thank you"

"I'm so happy you completed these intense training, thank you" said Gregg

"If you ever want to learn anything else you know where I am but some things take longer than others I spent one year mastering one skill so if you are not patient I don't recommend you doing some of the skills"

"Trust me I don't think I'll do this again" they both laugh together.

"Hey how about we go out for tea to celebrate

and catch up"

"That sounds great says gregg"

"Where do you want to go?" said Gregg

"How do you expect me to know where to go? I have not lived here for 20 years well there was one restaurant I used to love the buccaneer I used to go there with your mother when we were your age"

"Buccaneer never heard of it"

"Its probably been destroyed for new houses anyway that was down town"

"Alright we could go to the pizza place perfect I have not had pizza in ages buddhists believe in strict diet"

"Yeah how does your friends think about you leaving"

"They were fine with it"

"Alright lets make move"

"So how is life over in the himalayas"

"I contemplated going over there as a young boy I was just so fascinated by the mountains and once I got older I decided to move there but for a reason to learn the religion buddhism"

"cool"

"yeah it is pretty cool I guess" says Uncle Bill

"So have you got any stories Uncle Bill"

"wheel there was one time where I traveled up the snowy mountains of the himalayas and seen various different types of extraordinary animals such as mountain leopard bears elks if you don't know what they are they are reindeers basicly"

"So how about you what about your life Gregg well just a normal teenage lad" they both laugh.

Chapter 30

The force fields

Location:in gregs bedroom

Time: 13/03/2012 - 06:00pm

Gregg attempts to leave
"where do you think you are going"
"cant we go home Uncle Bill"
"once you have mastered it we can leave"
"I am leaving bye Uncle Bill"
"you cannot leave"

"Uncle Bill i cant keep going i am far too tired"

"stay and practice young one you must"

please Uncle Bill i need to leave i am exhausted i can't concentrate"

Uncle Bill summons a bucket of water and throws it over Gregg to wake him up a bit more.

"What was that for"

"you said you were tired so i refreshed you"

"I didn't want you to do that"

"well be more specific in the future"

Gregg attempts to leave again and Uncle Bill stops him.

"Wait Gregg i will make you a deal"

"Gregg shouts i am listening, so whats your deal"

"If you can break through this mighty force field i will let you leave but if you fail to break free you must stay and train"

So Harder than ever before Gregg pushed and pushed until the force field evaporated but the way it evaporated was some water from earlier was lying in a ditch so he cupped his hands and threw it all over a ghost to create an arch way.

Uncle Bill congratulated him for his wisdom and took him home.

Uncle Bill and Greg was sitting at a cafe waiting for their pepperoni pizza having a conversation about their powers and how long they have known for.

"Gregg tells Uncle Bill that he has known about his power for three years but told practically nobody, And Bill was privileged to be the first one to hear about it.

"You are really strong with magic kid always remember that"

Thier pizza is ready then they eat.

Chapter 31

Tipping Point

Location: out side

Time: 14/03/2012 - 08:00pm

Billy needs to come up with a plan to get revenge on some people so he chose to get revenge on the 3 boys.Billy went home that night to come up with a plan.If you knew billy you would know that he always succeeds in his evil bullying business and this is his bullying business so indeed he does succeed.So billy stayes up all night going overr the plan and making sure its makes scence and asking his self "is this plan gonna work out and succed".so he finally goes to bed to get some sleep at 12:00pm the next morning before he woke up at 5;00pm to work out his big evil plan.

So when billy got up to start his work on the plan he took all his thing down to the basement to work out the plan like what hes gonna need, whens he gonna do it, wheres he gonna do it, how hes gonna get the 3 boys to walk into it.SNAP it popped into billy's head how hes gonna do it, what's he gonna need etcetera but yet billy still needed to work out a couple of things so he set off into the bottom of town to get the answers to the questions that will help him set the evil plan for the 3 boys.billie then gets all the answers and questions and heads back home for tea before starting work again because all billy does is work on this plan to make sure its right and that hes definately gonna succeed at this plan, or he has chances of getting caught and he will get into lots and lots of trouble and maybe taken away from home.

After billys tea he goes back down town a second time to look at getting the equipment for his plan.He doesn't have any family but he does know some shops that he can go to where he can get a discount on the tools that he buys.Billy doesn't know if he will be able to get all the equipment that he needs to complete this plan but he does know that he will find a way to make it work and he will bully people until hes ready to stop because he want revenge for the people that bullied at his last school.When billy does end up getting all the equipment he needs he starts heading back up home again to get a new long sleep for setting up his plan tomorrow.

After billys good nights sleep he goes down to the basement where he kept his equipment and packed it all in the truck.He drove downtown to where the 3 boys lived with his things and house but house he set up the big plan but he always made sure nobody was around and nobody was home or he would easily get caught and took to jail which was something he was risking but didn't think it would actually go to the extent where he would get caught so he carried on with his plan at the 3 boys houses

Shortly after he arrived at his destination he tested his plan a couple times before getting the 3 boys involved.His plan wasn't going as he planned at first but after a couple times of testing he got there in the end.When billy finally succeeded at this evil plan he went off on a human scavenger hunt to find the 3 boys.Later that day he did find them and he asked them to play a game, they said yeah, so off the 4 boys went.Billys plan was going perfectly.The boys walked straight into billys plan.

Billy told them it was hide and seek but i wasn't, they were aloud to hide at peters house, louises house or greggs house, so thats exactly what they did.Gregg went to his house peter went to his house and louis went to his house.When they all got to their houses there was trappes and vandalism everywhere at all 3 houses, everyone from the streets to see the terrible damage that has been done to the 3 boys houses.Next the police came and billy was gone, the 3 boys found a note and it read "if u figure out who did this mess keep it to yourself, tell anyone and u will be beaten up and bullied for the rest of your time at high school" the boys then knew it was billy who done the vandalism to the houses.

Billys plan has not succeeded yet, he still needs to cover up the evidence and the trails that lead to billy, but billy was very smart when it came to evil bullying so he went home, done the maths and waited until the houses were clear before going back to the houses to clear up his tracks.He was not smart at all but right now he felt like the smartest boy on this earth.Never in this world and time was billy gonna be smarter than everyone and he knew that but he can still be smart at the things that he sets his mind to and if he works very hard at.

Chapter 32

the apology

Location:In St Patricks

Time: 17/03/2012 - 02:06pm

Louis was walking up the hill feeling sad and wanted someone to be his friend, just as he saw Peter, his spirit lifted. He sped up then started to run towards him. He ran across the road and took out his headphones then brought down his hood

As Louis ran towards Peter he called on him "Peter" he shouted, Peter lifted his head and he screwed his face up and shook it.

As soon as Peter lifted his face he started walking alongside the wall of the park and dropped his head to the floor, Peter could hear heavy, fast footsteps behind him like he always did when they were best mates, casing after each other like now. Louis finally caught up with Peter, Peter kept his head down and didn't say anything. Louis wanted to talk.

"What are you doing here, I thought you weren't talking to me, blanking me" Peter mumbled

Louis felt incredibly horrible for the way he treated him but he started shouting and screaming at him because he was angry and mad "Ok, you wanna why I was mean to you?" he asked un politely

"Why, tell me why" he screamed

"Because i was jealous, jealous of you and David, you didn't care about me anymore so I just Went away with Billy, just to annoy you. But I swear

I never meant to hurt you. Since he came you went with him so I went away with Billy, I'm so sorry....... I can understand if you don't want to be friends with me again" Louis slows down and stops to turn the other way when Peter says

"Wait" he said quietly "I'm sorry" Louis looked at him and turned around "I'm sorry for leaving you out, it's just there was a new boy, I wanted to welcome him, make him feel comfortable....."

"you didn't need to leave me out though" he yelled

"I know" he murmured "can we be friends again?"

They keep walking down the road until they get to a red ferrari, they both turn round to each other and Louis tells him " it hurt what you did.... but of course we can still be friends..... you're my best mate"

They both give each other a big hug and tell each other they missed not hanging out and being friends, Louis held him closely and taped his back Peter almost did the same but held his head instead. They stood there for five minutes enjoying the moment incase they never got that same feeling again, that feeling was excitement and having your best friend back.

They let go of each other and look at each other weirdly, they then clear their throats and hesitate on what to do or say next

"So" Louis breaking the silence and a sigh of relief from Peter "what's David like?"

"Em he's ok I guess, he likes video games, he's quite clingy though, like he follows me everywhere I mean I've told him my daily plan and he knows that I'm busy Monday, Wednesday, Friday but no he still decides to call me and ask if i want to do something"

"Wow calm down Peter"

"Sorry, I get really annoyed, I guess at the time I didn't want to show it incase I ended up with no one, he still my friend though"

"Um... why don't you tell me about mr bully" Peter laughed and Louis looked at him strangely

" Ok, what do you wanna know?" Said peter

"Anything" he said with a yawn at the end of

it

"Em... he's annoying and he's always calling me up to see if I want to go bully people, he likes video games, he is really clingy, ...he's dark and mean and i'm never going to be friends with him again" Louis looked as if he was going cry but Peter made him happy again by telling him "You know I think they're the perfect match of friends for each other" Louis thought for a moment " I mean think about it.... their both clingy, they always call when they're not meant to, they both like video games their perfect"

They start to tell each other memories when they were younger just to stop thinking about David and Billy. They both laugh at each other, they look... and smile. they start to then mess about on the way home, screaming and laughing, punching and kicking.

Chapter 33

Rough

```
Location: in the Dr's room

Time: 18/03/2012 - 12:00 noon
```

"I've known Dr Daines since world war three we were good friends I was a commander while Dr Baines was a doctor for the injured we didn't really talk when we were in the war.

"Dr Baines tried to save my brother when he got shot in an artery in his leg he pulled out the bullet and kept pressure on the wound but sadly my brother died several hours later I thanked Dr Baines for trying to save him".

Gillian and Dr Baines became good friends after the war had finished they started talking a lot and were getting to be close friends.

In the war Dr Baines was a doctor he saved many lives but many were lost he tried his hardest to save lives he even risked his own to save lives and was nearly killed. because a man with a rifle shot at him from about a mile away.

Gillian was a fighter along with her brother they protected our country and protected Dr Baines and the other doctors

When Gillion and Dr Baines got free time in the war they met up and talked. Gillian went to her brothers grave to say hi, then they went to have dinner time I was great because it was the only time when nobody was attacked.

The hospital in the war was old and dusty and it was raining so all the patient who came in and out dragged mud blood and other rubbish and dirt into and out the hospital so it was harder to run about trying to save people

While Gillian was fighting saving friends family and others she was still trying to get over the death of her brother, gillian was a brave fighter she did not stop even know her brother died she kept on fighting.

Gillian went back home to nobody because her husband sadly died and her brother in the war .

Dr Baines went back home and became a doctor helping people with mental issues.

Chapter 34

Rough and tumble

Location:in the street

Time: 18/03/2012 - 09:00am

Peter stops before he takes his medication and thinks to his self if he should take his medication or not he thinks to his self what would happen if he never took his medication or not what would happen to him if he never took it or not would get worse would it get better or would it stay or would it get worse so he decided to get rid of them he emptied his medication box and put them all in the bin. After that he went and put the tv on and watched the football scores from the week as he was doing that he got a thought in his head i need the tablets i want to get better i want to get rid of it so peter got up and went to the bin and opened it and took them out and put them back in the box why he was doing his mum joyce came in the house and walked through with the shopping and saw peter raking in the bin and peters mum asked "what are you doing in the bin peter", Peter jumps in fear and replies "oh mum you gave me a fright "

mum replied "sorry son but what are you doing in the bin" peter replies anxiously

"erm nothing mum i think i chucked the tv battery away earlier on" mum replies

"ok but remember and wash your hands once you have found it ok" peter replied

"yes no bother mum will clean them in a minute" mum replies

"ok no bother son" mum leaves the room and goes and watches the tv.

Peter says to his self "few that was a close one mum could of caught me" peter gets all the medication out the bin and goes and puts it back in the medication box.

Chapter 35

Storms

Location:in the jail

Time: 20/03/2012 - 04:00pm

Everyone started to look at him, they all looked shocked.The judge was not pleased with Billy's behaviour.The judge says to Billy "I do not hope to see you back here ever again". Billy realized that he was in a lot of trouble and he regretted what he had done. Billy never thought that he would ever do something like this or ever end up in the mess he was in, but he then knew he was in too much trouble to take back the damage he had done.

Everyone wanted the chance to ask Billy questions about what he had done and why he did it because nobody really understands. Lots of people in the court want answers and Billy knows this, Billy knows he's going to have to go through this day telling answers to the questions that he thought he would never have to think about. Billy doesn't really understand why he done such a bad thing when he could have just accepted the facts that he had a fall out with Louis but he doesn't really like accepting facts that he doesn't like. He feels anger, pain, depression and lots more but yet he refuses to talk to someone which is maybe why Billy has ended up in this situation.

He already knew that if he got caught this was a possibility, but he didn't expect it to end up in court or in jail, so he did as he was asked to, he answered all the questions that he could from his family and the 4 boys.He said he was sorry and he regretted what he had done to the boys and it was just then that he told them the real reason he done the vandalizing.Billy told them that the reason he vandalized all 4 houses was because they were all back together again and he was very very upset about getting left out.

As Billy always gets worked up and stuff well he did but this time because he realised the trouble he was in, he found a way to calm down, get over it and get back to the court case nice and easy or he would have been in a lot more trouble than he was already is, and if he was to get into anymore trouble there will be a longer jail sentence and maybe a deeper fine. He might not be allowed to go back to school if he gets into anymore trouble.

He got very nervous when he found out he was gonna have to start answering to the police but he knew if he done one thing out of line today it can affect everything that happens and any other future day. When the police asked Billy the first question he started shaking, getting nervous and scared but he knew this had to be done and he couldn't plead guilty because the is proof that he is guilty and he knew that if he got caught lying he would be in EVEN MORE TROUBLE.

Before he answered to the judge he started getting very upset and emotional. Billy never thought he would have to answer questions that the judge had or that the judge even had questions but he did and no matter what happened billy had to answer to the judge because he was the most important person that Billy had to answer to. Finally the judge made her decision.

He got put into jail with a jail mate for 4 years, a year for each person he hurt and affected.(Louis, Gregg, Peter and David). He thought he was gonna go back and finish school but he would be in jail too long and won't be allowed to go back...after the 4 years was up he would be allowed to go back and finish the last year at school, but along with the 4 years in prison he got fined 500 pounds

THE END

Made in the USA
Charleston, SC
16 February 2015